Ted Bear's
Magic Swing

By Dianne Baker

Illustrated by Ronda Krum

Unity Books
Unity Village, MO 64065 USA

A **Wee Wisdom**®
Book.

Illustrated by Ronda Krum
Text and cover designed by Tom Hubbard

Copyright © 1992 by Dianne Baker

All Rights Reserved
LLC 91-065819
ISBN 0-87159-162-6
Canada GST R132529033

This book is printed on recycled paper.

Acknowledging the gentle, guiding Presence within, Ted Bear lovingly dedicates this story to each reader and sends a very special thank-you to his Auntie Mag for her encouragement and assistance in bringing his story to publication.

Every day, just after lunch, Ted Bear went to swing in his swing.

Now Ted Bear's swing was a simple one, made of rope and a flat piece of wood. The ends of the rope were tied around a wonderful, thick branch of his favorite tree. And his favorite tree was in a quiet corner of the woods.

Ted Bear would swing—up and down, back and forth, high and low and high again—leaning his feet way out. He loved the way the wind blew first in his face, then at his back.

This was always a special time of day for Ted Bear—a time just for him. When he was in his swing, Ted Bear wouldn't think about chores he had to do or places he needed to go. He would just look at the beautiful sky, the trees, and his feet. He would just swing.

Maybe it seems that Ted Bear had nothing to do all day except swing. But Ted Bear was really a very busy bear, with lots of chores to do and lots of places to go.

You see, Ted Bear was in charge of the honey supply for all the bears in the forest. He had to buy the honey from the bees, find a place to store it, and then make sure that all the bears got their share. It was a very important job!

But Ted Bear always got his work done, and had a very good time doing it too. That was because of the magic in his swing.

One day some of the animals asked Ted Bear why he always seemed so happy and where he got all the wonderful ideas he was always coming up with. Ted Bear scratched his head and thought a minute.

Finally he said, "It has to be because I take time every day, just after lunch, to swing in my swing. Maybe you should try it too."

But the animals just laughed. "We are all too busy to swing, Ted Bear. We have too much work to do!"

But Ted Bear knew something they didn't know. He knew that swinging helped him relax, and relaxing helped his brain work better the other times of the day.

"Too bad the others won't try it," he said. "I think they'd be surprised."

Then one afternoon while Ted Bear was on his way to visit the bees, he ran into Sarah Beaver. Today was Sarah's day to watch all the baby beavers in the woods while their mothers and fathers built new dams for the ponds.

Beavers are always very busy, but baby beavers seem to be even busier! Poor Sarah was running here and running there, trying to keep up with all the babies.

"Hi, Sarah," said Ted Bear. "How are you today?"

"Oh, Ted! I'm getting so tired. I wish there were some way to keep the babies from getting into so much mischief. I never know what they'll be up to next."

Just then, Sam Squirrel came racing by, his arms full of acorns.

"Hi, Sam," called Ted Bear. "Why are you in such a hurry?"

"I have to collect lots of acorns today, and I'm running late. Barney was supposed to help me, but he's sick." Sam started scampering from tree to tree.

"Hey, wait, Sam!" said Ted Bear. "I have an idea."

Ted Bear called Sarah Beaver and Sam Squirrel together and talked to them.

A short time later, Sarah was swinging in Ted Bear's swing—up and down, back and forth, high and low and high again.

When she had finished, Sarah was happy and relaxed and ready to go back to the baby beavers.

When she returned to the babies, they were still scurrying around, helping Sam Squirrel in his acorn hunt. A big pile of acorns lay on the ground.

"This was a great idea," said Sam to Sarah. "Look how many acorns we collected while you were swinging! And the babies think it's a game. Just look at them."

"Now it's your turn, Sam," said Sarah. "We'll keep collecting acorns for you while you swing. You'll be glad you took time for it."

A few minutes later, Sam Squirrel was swinging in Ted Bear's swing. When he stopped, he felt much better, and his mind was filled with new ideas about all kinds of things.

So that was how Sam and Sarah learned the secret of Ted Bear's swing. But there were still those in the woods who thought taking time to swing each day was a silly waste of time.

Then one summer day, a thunderstorm came through the woods. Ted Bear thought the lightning and thunder made a pretty good show. Besides, the rain filled the streams and ponds with fresh water and watered all the meadows and the flowers.

Now this storm was pushed along on its way by a wind—a wind that ruffled the trees and everything else that happened to be in its path. Unfortunately, on this day the bees' honey factory, which was not fastened securely to its tree, was ruffled right down to the ground!

This was terrible. Without the honey factory, the bees wouldn't be able to make their honey to sell to Ted Bear.

After the storm and the ruffling wind had passed, Ted Bear went to see the damage and talk to the bees about what could be done.

The bees told Ted Bear it could be weeks before a new factory could be built. Several bears who were standing nearby groaned and grumbled. They were afraid Ted Bear might not have enough honey stored up to last until the factory was rebuilt.

"Can't you use *this* factory?" asked Ted Bear.

"No," said the head bee. "It has to be way up there in that tall tree. And we could never move this one. We'll have to build a brand-new factory."

But Ted Bear knew there had to be an answer to this problem, if he could only think of it.

He told the bees and the bears to wait a bit, then he went alone to his favorite tree and his swing. As he moved— up and down, back and forth, high and low and high again— he relaxed and watched the clouds.

Soon, two ideas came to him. He hopped out of his swing and got busy.

First, he stopped to watch the forest spiders building a web. The spiders were well respected for their construction skills.

"Can I talk to you for a minute?" Ted Bear asked the head spider. He explained his idea to the spider.

In no time, the spiders were busy working in the tree that the honey factory had fallen from. They were building strong supports for the factory to be fastened to.

Soon there was nothing left to do but fasten the factory back into the tree.

"But how will we ever get it up there?" asked the head bee. "It's impossible!"

"No, I don't think so," said Ted Bear. "While the spiders were busy, I spoke to some of the birds. Here they come now!"

"All finished!" called the birds together, as they dropped a net near the honey factory. They had been busy weaving the net from twigs and vines. It was very strong.

"Now, if some of you bears will very carefully lift the factory onto the net," said Ted Bear, "the birds will fly it up into the tree, and the squirrels and spiders can work together to get it fastened tightly in place."

Soon the honey factory was back in its tree. The bees were sure they could repair the damage from the fall in a short time.

"Hurray for Ted Bear!" cried the bears. They were very relieved that they wouldn't be running out of honey.

"Hurray for my swing," said Ted Bear, and he explained again about how his ideas had come.

The spiders asked Ted Bear if they could swing in his swing, and Ted Bear led them into the quiet corner of the woods. The bees came along to watch.

Now the spiders, being so small, could not make the swing move at all. Ted Bear was ready to give them a push when the bees decided they could help by pushing and pulling the ropes of the swing for the spiders. The spiders and the bees had such a good time they agreed to meet every day to swing!

By now, the animals were beginning to suspect that Ted Bear was right about his swing. Sarah and Sam were happier. The bees buzzed more merrily. Everyone said the spiders' webs were more beautiful and unusual than any they had ever seen.

Each day, more and more of the animals lined up for a turn in Ted Bear's swing. There wasn't always enough time for everyone to have a turn.

But that was a problem that was *easy* to solve.

Soon there were swings all over the forest so everyone could take time, every day, just to be alone and swing—up and down, back and forth, high and low and high again!